Louise Sayger, MD

SIX DAYS
Inside A Mountain

SIX DAYS

Inside A Mountain

Louane K Beyer

Illustrations by Hilbert Bermejo

along with Roger Beyer and grandchildren, Emilee
Lindseth, Adam Beyer, Abigail Beyer and Allie Beyer

To order additional copies of this book, contact:
Xlibris Corporation
1-888-795-4274
www.Xlibris.com
Orders@Xlibris.com

ACKNOWLEDGEMENTS:

THANK YOU TO my husband, Roger, and our grandchildren Emilee, Adam, Abigail, Allie and Nathan for their encouragement, ideas and illustrations. Also I appreciated the support of the children's moms, Laurie and Lisa. To the illustrators at Xlibiris for their assistance in the illustrations.

Plus appreciation for the hobby of ham radio which has been an integral part of my life for over thirty years. Amateur radio communications is a service of self trained technical radio operators who are comprised of people from all walks of life who share interest in radio technique. A requirement is to attain a valid FCC amateur license which when earned is a special achievement. "Hams" as we are called provide a voluntary, noncommercial communication service which is especially important during national disasters or emergencies through the international morse code and sometimes voice. In our family, we have 4 operators in the extra class and one in the technical class. We have volunteered in activities such as Sky Warn, training, disaster drills plus the challenge of international contacts. Equipment can range from portable to high tech radios to access frequency bands. For myself as an extra class license involved learning about radio waves, operating standards, electrical principles, circuit components, and morse code. I also liked the opportunity to learn new skills.

CONTENTS

DAY 1

Tuesday August 12

IT WAS EARLY in the morning with the sun barely peeking over the horizon as Peter stretched while waking up. He was excited as he remembered that yesterday, August 11, had been his 13th birthday with his parents surprising him by giving him a pellet rifle. His dad, who worked as a construction engineer, was also an avid hunter and had taken Peter on several trips into the nearby mountains to hunt rabbits and deer for the family to eat. They lived close to a chain of mountains that was part of the Rocky Mountains where there was ample game. The rifle was a good beginning to practice for larger hunts so his dad had given him permission to walk into the foothills to try out his new rifle and to take his ten-year-old brother, Andy, with him. That suited Peter just fine as he and Andy were amiable brothers.

He remembered that his dad had given him strict instructions on how far they could go. He asked them to use precautions so neither of them would get hurt. Along with this, Peter had been a boy scout for many years and had learned about being trust worthy.

But all that fell to the wayside as he jumped out of bed to get ready to go shoot some squirrels or maybe even a rabbit. He called for Andy to get out of bed. His mom was cooking breakfast as Peter entered the kitchen. She was anxious this morning as she did not like what the boys were going to do that day. It was several miles away and she worried that something could happen. Brad had assured her that Peter was responsible and would see that Andy stayed safe also. They had been urged to be back by 4:30 that afternoon. It was only three weeks before school started and there was soccer practice at 5:30. Peter enjoyed the practice so he assured his dad and mom the night before that they would be back long before then.

His mom had prepared some oatmeal and toast with some fresh berry jam. She had been berry picking in the foothills over the last weekend using them to make some fresh jam. Both Peter and Andy ate well. Peter asked his mom if she would fix them each a peanut butter and jam sandwich to take along while they checked their back packs before the excursion. Peter took a quick look in his back pack to make sure he had his tin can with the ammo in it and a canister of water. He called to Andy to be sure to take some fresh water and some snacks from Mom as well. It was a sunny day so they wore light shirts. They each tucked a sweat shirt into the pack then waved to their mom and sister as they trudged off to the foothills. It was 8:00 in the morning with the sun already getting hot. They both wore caps to shield the sun that was beating down on them. They didn't go very far before Andy said he was thirsty already. He took a swig of the cool water.

Neither talked very much as they walked along looking for some targets that Peter could use. It seemed like the birds were all gone and there was no activity in the underbrush. They kept walking getting involved in searching the tall grasses looking for wildlife of some sort. The sun kept getting hotter. Both of the boys seemed to be in a trance as they walked looking around. Neither noticed that land had started to rise leaving the flat lands behind them.

By 12:00 they had walked several miles and were getting sort of weak. Andy asked if they could stop to eat and rest. Peter agreed that this was a good idea. They found a shaded area to get out a half of a sandwich and then drink some water. They rested on the ground under a giant aspen tree.

Peter told Andy about what he thought he would do if he shot a rabbit that day. He had his knife with him and could skin it. After some thought, he said that he would probably hook it on his back pack and do that at home. His excitement returned as he jumped up to go grabbing Andy by his shirt lightly pulling him to his feet. They heard some scurrying and became involved in following the sound.

Peter quietly said for Andy to stay close behind him so that if he had to raise his rifle he would know that Andy was behind him. They crept along being ever so quiet. Neither noticed where they were going nor what direction they had taken. The sound of what they were following had stopped. Peter asked Andy if he thought the small animal had perhaps gone up into a tree. He offered that Andy should look around the ground to see if it had gone under a root or into a hole while he would look up the evergreen tree. They went several more yards then tracked back. It was so quiet. Time had slipped away with Andy now saying he was getting cool. He was going to take out his sweatshirt to put on. Peter looked at his watch and was taken aback. He could hardly believe that it read 4:30.

He looked around seeing only big Ponderosa and Fir trees. Where were they he wondered? How far had they gone from where they had eaten their sandwich? He un-cocked his rifle and sat down to get his bearings. He thought of climbing a tree to look around then realized they were too big and too thick to climb.

They were lost. He had forgotten all his dad had told him. He broke the trust that his dad had placed with him. The trees all seemed the same with the sunlight fading. What were they to do? He knew that he must do the very utmost to protect Andy and looked over at him. He saw that Andy was thinking the same. They were lost and would need to take steps to protect themselves.

They were under a canopy of trees and could make the most of it but they knew that wasn't good enough. They talked about how they should have been looking for markers to which they would have referred to in order to find the way back. That was useless now. They decided to look around a bit to see where they were and what they could use to set up a camp.

This was not what Peter had learned in scouts. There was a set plan with counselors guiding the group of boys. The boys would chat and push each other around until it was time to get their assigned tasks completed. For now, Peter did not want to think of the times he had with the boy scouts and the security of the pack leaders.

The brothers walked around holding each other's hand

for fear they would lose track of each other as that was unbearable to imagine. One tree looked like another with the branches close to the ground so it was not a good choice to make a bed for them. The ground was filled with tree roots, heavy pine needles and hard soil. It even seemed like the ground was wet. What would keep them dry they asked each other?

Peter put thoughts of the whopping his dad would give him for all the worry that he had caused. For now though, he had to remain strong. He kept looking around for a safe place to make a bed along with a small clearing to build a fire. That was going to be the major priority as they needed the fire for safety while not setting the woods on fire. Finally they located the spot then began to cut some branches to make a sort of lean-to in which they could sleep.

Then Peter told Andy that they needed to gather a lot of small twigs plus some larger ones to keep the fire going all night. Once this task was accomplished, they set to look around at what was in the area. This time though they mentally marked the way they went to so they would know how to get back to this place. It was getting darker but Peter felt the need to search what was nearby.

They didn't walk very far when they came upon a cave. The opening wasn't too big but they could easily get into it.

They stooped to peer into it to see if it went deep into the mountain. The cave looked dark and sort of scary at least at this time of day. Both boys looked but couldn't make out anything. Peter said, "I wonder if there are any big animals in there hiding out." Andy shook his head thinking that this is one place that he would like to avoid if at all possible. In fact, he wanted to get as far away from it as possible.

For now though, they hurried back to their site which would be their home for the night. After looking at the cave, they both felt some comfort in the site they had chosen to spend the night. They built a small fire which warmed them both with the heat and the bright light it gave off. All of a sudden, Peter realized his selfishness. Looking at his smaller brother sitting next to him, Peter became frightened of how he had only thought of himself and his new gun. There was Andy shaking with big tears coming to his eyes. He put his arm around Andy then asked him if he was thinking of home.

Andy leaned into him and told him that he could picture how worried and scared Mom and Dad would be. They would wonder if both of their sons were hurt or worse dead. Peter told him that he was thinking the same. He told Andy that he had been so thoughtless by not paying any attention to where they were going, determined only to aim his rifle at some animal to shoot it.

He also felt he wanted to cry but reminded himself that he must remain strong in spirit for Andy. He told Andy that tomorrow dad would get the Rangers to fly over the area and arrange for people to help with the search for them. There were many guys who hunted up here and were familiar with the territory enabling them to be rescued. This helped to reassure Andy. Soon he stopped shaking.

Andy gulped and said he was hungry. This encouraged Peter so he bent over to reach into his backpack to bring out a half of sandwich which he shared with Andy. It helped some but Peter was still so hungry. Andy ate his small piece without saying anything but Peter knew he was still hungry also.

Visions of what might have been came to his head as he thought that if he had been more observant in watching the trees and the paths, they could be at home right now. Mom would be cooking supper, sister doing coloring at the kitchen table, Dad on his way home with both Andy and himself warm and secure. Instead here they were lost in the mountains and in danger for sure. He tried not to think of the enormity of the situation he had put them both in.

Peter tried to make them both feel better by telling some

boy scout and hunting stories. He reached into his back pack for the flashlight and turned it on. He felt good that it was shining brightly but he turned it off quickly to save battery power as he did not know how much they would need it. He tucked Andy into their lean-to where he immediately fell asleep.

Peter knew he had to stay awake all night to keep the fire going to protect them. He heard so many strange sounds and rustling going on. He imagined what animals they were and what they looked like. He kept putting small pieces of wood on the fire while watching the flames. He began getting sleepy. He knew that just couldn't happen. He tried to remember happy times by recalling memories that would keep him awake. It started to rain. He was stricken with even more fear as they had no rain gear. He couldn't crawl into the lean-to fearing that the fire would go out. He brought out his sweatshirt and found a plastic bag in his pocket which he put over the top of his head to keep it dry. He tucked his cap into the backpack to keep it dry.

Thinking back to more memories, he thought of his room at home. That cheered him a bit. It was painted a lime green color with bland shades and burgundy drapes that he had helped to pick out. On the walls he had pasted posters of all kinds of Star Wars and space ships. He often let his imagination bring them to life as he lay on his bed day dreaming. He thought of the painting that his Grandmother had done for him. It was a print of two wolves in a night scene. He wondered if he would actually see the same type of wolf here in the mountains.

The room itself was messy and that was how he liked it. Even this morning, he had left the wet towel on the floor after he had showered in his anxiousness to get going. He now thought that his mom must have shaken her head during the day as she passed his room seeing that. He thought she would make a mental note to remind Peter that he should throw towels and dirty clothes in the hamper. It brought him some comfort to think of his dear mom and how much they were loved and cared for by her. Then there were his favorite objects which were placed in the room on the shelves where he kept all his treasures and boxes with small items in them. There were trophies from his years as a cub scout then as a boy scout. He was really good with his sling shot and in his mind, took it off the shelf and stretched the band across the frame and aimed it. Poof! Poof! As it snapped back.

There were some rock and shell collections that he had gathered on the many different places they had camped. His grandfather had a wide assortment of rocks and fossils which helped create the interest in them. Then there were some photos of himself, his friends and his family. He did not want to think in that direction as he was near crying so his thoughts came back to his room and his bed which had a really cool comforter with deer, trees and outdoor scenes on it. He and his dad had picked out the regular size bed with a head board where he could set some of his things like his baseball and Pokemon cards that he had collected, his blood flashlight that he now wished he had with him which would offer a bright light, some books and the necklace he had made from pop tops of cans strung on a chain from his mom, and so many more.

The bed had a space under it with drawers that he could store more of his objects. So cool! Oh if he could be there now. Instead his mind moved to his bookshelves that were filled with his favorite books and magazines. He closed his eyes to picture the names of the books and how they were neatly arranged on the shelves. He remembered his scout book and tried very hard to remember some of the chapters on survival. All this helped to calm him as he thought of some of the skills he had learned in scouts. This helped to ward off the sleep which was weighing heavy on his tired and sore body.

He thought that he would share his remembrances with Andy in the morning. Andy was quietly breathing as he slept and Peter took comfort that he was acting like the brother he should have been earlier in the day. He loved Andy so much and vouched to himself that he would put Andy's needs ahead of his own but also remembering that he had to take care of himself also for the family's sake. As he sat there trying so hard to stay awake, his head nodded again in sleep. He heard a strange noise and growling close by. He quickly put some more small pieces of wood on the fire and sat back. His heart was pounding.

He was terribly frightened. Could this be the wolves that he had thought of a few minutes ago? He knew there were animals as wolves, bears and cougars up here in the mountains.

These were animals he had only seen in a zoo, in magazines or on television. Whatever it was could attack at any moment so he sat very still waiting. He heard more rustling with the animal growling coming closer. He could sense that it was big.

He became braver by putting more wood on the fire worrying that the supply would not last the night as he had already used a portion of it. This was not a time to spare wood though.

The growling became fainter as the animal must have moved on from the fear of the fire. Soon with the danger past, Peter's head nodded and he fell into a deep, deep sleep. He dreamed that he heard his brother calling him. Andy kept shaking Peter calling out his name with alarm in his voice. "Peter, Peter wake up, wake up, there is a big fire and the wind is whipping the flames up into the trees," Andy shouted as he kept shaking Peter without waking him. He shook him again. This time he seemed to respond as Andy repeatedly called out, "Help! Help!" Peter jumped up and couldn't believe his eyes at what he was seeing. He looked around and saw that the campfire had spread to the big evergreens with the wind stirring the flames into the branches. Sparks were flying all around. This caused his eyes to burn and he could hardly see. He saw Andy running around trying to beat out the flames with a branch without success. The sound was deafening to his ears.

Peter took the plastic bag off his hair, stuck it in his pocket then grabbed Andy by the arm along with the two backpacks and headed away from the lean-to. He couldn't think of what to do but knew he must control the wild thoughts in order to save them.

The only safe place from the heat, the flames, the sound and the fire was the cave. He motioned for Andy to stay close

to him as a big Ponderosa exploded into flames. Peter pulled Andy closer. With heads bent down, they moved away from the lean-to area with Peter dragging the two backpacks. They struggled to save their lives by running to the entrance of the cave.

As they crawled into the entrance of the cave, they found the surface to be mostly sand. A cool breeze hit them. It was easier to breathe with the two of them taking a deep breath.

There was some light from the fire raging outside so they were comforted that they did not have to sit in the dark or use their flashlights which they did not want to except in case of an emergency.

What had earlier seemed to them a dark hole in the mountain now was a place of refuge. At least for the time being, they were in a safe place. Desolation set in as both Peter and Andy wondered how they were to survive. Their stomachs were growling as hunger set in. The question both of them asked themselves was what were they going to eat? They had one sandwich left and now with the fire raging outside, it would be almost impossible to look for food.

As the crackling continued outside, Andy offered that they should focus on what would their dad do in this case. Andy remembered in times of crisis dad would remain calm and talk about options on how to get them through. He shared these with Peter who thought for a while then agreed. He also remembered how mom liked to make lists. They could set priorities.

Peter remembered that he had assured Andy that their dad would be organizing a search party to find them. He was skeptical now as he wondered how horses and four wheelers would get through the flames. A helicopter would be hampered by the high winds and the heavy smoke. He looked at Andy and told him what he felt was the reality of the situation. Andy agreed. Andy told Peter that he was really hungry. They needed food for strength. Peter asked Andy to find some munchies that he had suggested for him to bring along. They quickly devoured one packet. Peter told Andy what he had thought about as he had sat by the fire during the night. He had remembered some of the tips that the Scout leaders had stressed which were roots and berries.

They had spent many hours teaching the boys what was edible and what was bitter. They had gone over pictures, drawings and even real ones. Then he spoke of going out of the cave. At first he said that he wanted to go alone but then they were in this together.

Andy agreed that together was better. He trusted Peter. With this accomplished, Peter brought out his knife and pulled the plastic bag from his pocket. The same plastic bag he had used to keep his head dry from the showers. It seemed like so long ago that he had been sitting by the fire thinking while Andy had been sleeping. Peter took a deep breath. He told Andy to do that also as they were heading back outside into the heat, the flames and the wind.

Then strapping his back pack on, he then advised Andy to do the same. They did not want to take the chance of losing their back packs as it was all they had at this time. Peter picked up his rifle as he thought it could be useful in the outside. Slowly they crept on their hands and knees to the cave opening. They felt the tremendous, intense heat from the fire. It was so scary. They became mesmerized by how high the red flames from the evergreen and cottonwood trees were shooting into the sky. They almost crawled backwards into the cave but remembered how hungry they were. They continued outward. Peter led the way going cautiously as he did not want to take the chance of burning branches falling on them. He worried that a tree could fall and block the entrance to the cave. He observed what was happening and then proceeded. Just outside the entrance, he reached for Andy's hand to help him stand up. As they crouched low against the mountain's stone wall, they inched their way along.

Several feet out, they lucked out and found a small crevasse with some berry bushes that the fire hadn't reached. They both stuffed their mouths full relishing the flavor and the juice while spitting out the stone pits.

Oh how good it was to eat something. They filled their pockets and the plastic bag with the berries. The nourishment gave them strength. They slowly worked their way back along the stone wall crawling on their knees to enter the cave.

The sounds from the fire still roaring in their ears. They sat down close to the entrance of the cave feeling so much better now that they had eaten and had a reserve of food besides the sandwich.

It was cool in the cave. Andy suggested that Peter take a nap as he knew how tired Peter was. He offered to stand guard by watching the entrance to the cave and the dark side that neither of them could imagine what was back there or where it led to. Peter agreed that he needed some rest. He laid his head on his backpack and immediately fell asleep. Andy stayed alert for any noises or sounds coming from the back of the cave. As he sat looking both ways, he wondered how deep it was, where it went to or if there were any animals that would come crashing out. He knew from school and some books he had read that some of these caves went deep into the mountains. Some caves were dark and dank with some completely void of any life while others had streams running through them. The study of caves had not really been a part of the geography he studied so far. Usually caves were areas that were good to avoid. His mind wandered for awhile as the thought of the caves took away the thoughts of what they were experiencing here. He watched over Peter lying beside him on the sand fast asleep.

Peter slept for about an hour awakening with a start wondering where he was. As he sat up, Andy assured him that they were ok here in the cave and safe for awhile from the flames and the fire. They each took a sip of the precious supply of water. Andy had emptied his pockets full of berries. Just having the berries close by gave him a good feeling. The berries seemed to calm him and settle the hunger that he had felt. He took great care not to crush them or drop them on the sand. He smiled at his brother telling him that at least now they had some food.

DAY 2

Wednesday August 13

PETER FELT BETTER after his short nap. It seemed to restore his ability to see what was happening and begin to plan for what needed to be done next. After talking about this, they decided this was a good time to do an assessment of what supplies or tools they had. They had light from the fire outside which made flickering shadows on the walls of the cave. This helped as they could see what they were doing while saving their flashlight batteries.

They opened their backpacks bringing the items out one by one. Peter began with his bag. They had little time to spare as they did not know how much longer they had light available.

The first item was the flashlight. Andy followed suit by bringing out his flashlight which he tested. It still had full power so he quickly turned it off. Each laid out what they had on the sand floor of the cave. After the packs were emptied, they studied what they had. Each had a water bottle half full. Peter had the Boy Scout cooking kit with the scout manual in the case. He was now grateful to have remembered to leave the book in the back pack. They had 2 pocket knives, granola bags, some tootsie rolls, pieces of venison jerky, a long piece of rope, some pieces of twine, several band aids, a few pieces of tin foil, 2 pairs of socks, 2 packs of matches, one P & J sandwich, a scout bandana, 2 caps, a candy bar, a small bottle of aspirin, 2 small bottles of antiseptic hand cleaner and a wad of paper towels in the bottom of each pack. Also Peter had the tin of ammo for his rifle.

Peter immediately wrapped each of the boxes of matches in a piece of tin foil to keep them dry stuffing them in a side pocket of each of the back packs. They both looked at the last sandwich and decided to eat it while it was fresh. It could dry up easily then what a waste that would be. Peter was happy to see the pieces of jerky. He remembered that they had helped dad make it after a recent hunt.

It would sustain them for quite awhile if no other sources of food were available with both of them now knowing what supplies they had and what they would need to look for. In addition, he felt secure that he had his pellet rifle and ammo which could be used to secure some wildlife meat. He was certain that most of the animals would have left the area due to the fire to find a safe place for themselves and their families. Visions of deer, cougar, bear and the small animals as well were moving about to be safe. The story about the fire in the book of Bambi came to mind with the huge fire and what it caused to the wildlife.

He shuttered when he thought of the chaos the fire was causing knowing that it was himself who had started it all with his selfishness and carelessness. The damage to not only the forest and the animals but also to the Rangers who would need to fight for their lives to put it out or contain it to a small area. He sat there quietly thinking of all of this unable to even share the thoughts of shame with his brother.

Andy was quiet for awhile finally admitting to Peter that they may not get rescued. Dad would not be able to find them here in this remote area. The Rangers would likely already be fighting the forest fire but would be starting at the lower rim working their way up. No one really knew where they were. An image came to Andy which he shared with Peter that he wondered if the Rangers would probably think that they had started the fire on purpose to let someone know where they were. Their dad would defend them.

Peter sighed and agreed to what Andy just voiced. He just couldn't even bring up the subject of what he had just run through his mind of who started all this and the guilt that he felt. He shook his head as if to clear the thoughts that were there. He needed to concentrate on the two of them. It was time to make more preparations as they only had a bottle of water. They could survive several days on what they had to eat but not without water.

So with great urgency, they talked of going out again and looking for more food for them to eat before they both kind of knew what the next step would be. A sort of calmness came over both of them as they put what had happened behind themselves.

So after storing the berries in a hole in the sand, they ventured outside again following the same method and path they had used before. Again Peter took his rifle along just in case there was a chance some small animal might jump out. He wanted to be ready. They stayed close to the ground backed by the stone wall as they crept towards the crevasse. The fire was so hot but they continued to search for necessities. Peter dug for some roots while Andy picked more berries. Andy filled the plastic bag again plus the scout cooking utensil along with all of his pockets. Peter put the roots in his pockets.

They returned to the cave to take their store there and rest for awhile as the trips were robbing them of what little energy they had. The sandwich had helped ease the hunger pangs. They put aside all thoughts of eating any more food as they were going to save anything else for later on. The sense of urgency was stronger than the need to replenish their energy. As they sat there, they talked about what to look for on the next trip out. They planned to drag in some tree branches if they could find some that weren't scorched by the flames.

After resting a bit, they set out to go again. Luckily, they located some branches that the wind had torn off and were still in useable shape. Just as they were sliding along the stone wall dragging the branches, they heard a noise. Peter reached for his rifle and cocked it ready to shoot whatever it was. They couldn't believe their eyes as it was a small rabbit that tried to scurry away. Quickly Peter aimed but missed. His hands were shaking so much. After taking a deep breath, he aimed and fired again hitting the rabbit in the head. Andy jumped on it just to make sure it wouldn't get up to hop away. Peter came closer and saw that it was dead.

He felt great pride in his accomplishment plus now they had a source of meat. As they crawled back into the cave dragging in the branches and the rabbit, they gave each other a high sign. For now just the meat they had was enough to create a bit of euphoria. It was like a good sign for both of them. Peter said, "The rabbit was probably hiding in the boughs in the crevasse to avoid getting burned by the fire. Whatever though, I am lucky to have shot it." Andy agreed that it was a good sign for them and smiled about it.

They had to rest for awhile again then got up to clean the rabbit. They took out their knives from their packs to tackle the project. Using their Swiss Army knives, they set to work. The first thing was to look for a flat rock in the cave. Andy searched around and located one. Then while he held the rabbit's legs one at a time against the rock, Peter dis-jointed the foot from the leg. Peter cut around the skin at the neck-line full circle. Then he cut the entire length of the rabbit starting from the cut at the neckline. This allowed them to gut the rabbit.

Andy then located a small twig using it to roll the skin back from the body of the rabbit. He remembered that their dad just pulled it off. Someday when he was stronger, he could do that also. Then they used some leaves to wipe off the meat. They wrapped the meat in a piece of tin foil. After that they used the antiseptic to clean their hands and the knives. The fur would have been saved and cured if they were at home. Even the feet of the rabbit could have been used as a good luck charm to make a Rabbit's Foot.

For now, they needed to dispose of the remains and crawled out of the cave to toss it far away to get burned. The area had to be cleaned very thoroughly with the sand scraped to avoid the chance that a cougar or other animal would be attracted to the scent of blood. Peter cut some of the toughest boughs he could sort out to make two supports with a cross bar to hold the rabbit in order to cook the meat.

It didn't work so he decided to build a small fire outside of the cave to cook the rabbit in one of the sparse pieces of tin foil he had. This would work. There would not be any odor in the cave.

He and Andy carefully crawled out of the cave to scrape together some wood to roast the rabbit. There were sufficient embers and the paper towels used to clean the rabbit so they did not need to use any matches. They gathered several rocks and laid the tin foil package on it. With this completed, they continued with their objective to gather more food. Soon the air became permeated with the odor of the meat as it was cooking. It made them so hungry but they continued the pursuit of collecting whatever they could use.

Peter was making mental notes of what to retrieve from the crevasse trying to recall what there was on the ground. He remembered some tall grass growing under the branches. He could gather that while Andy tackled finding more useable pine cones and nuts. The fire was too intense to look for birds or bird nests. He did want to try to scrape off some sap from the small evergreens in the crevasse. He could put it into a piece of tin foil. He didn't know why but felt it was important to collect the sap. Somewhere in the back of his mind, he pictured what would be next. Soon they would need to go deeper into the cave to look for water but that invoked darkness in his mind so he left it there. It was supposed to be day break according to his watch. He knew it was morning by the time on his watch but not by any conditions around him.

There was only darkness along with the stench of heavy smoke, black clouds and flames continuing shooting skyward. Peter's eyes burned as the wind whipped around the ashes. He turned to look at Andy seeing that he was experiencing the same condition. Andy came closer and said that yesterday at this time; they were at home sleeping in their beds. How could so much have happened in a few hours, not even a whole day. Both of them knew that this was their last trip outside. They had to be vigilant while rushing to gather all they could. They found pine nuts from the Pinon Tree, pine cones, tree bark and even uncovered a wild flower hidden under the stems of grass that Peter tore off, and last he scraped off more sap. They filled their arms with twigs and branches then tied them with the rope and twine. As they crawled back into the cave, they were totally exhausted.

Still to do was to retrieve the baking rabbit meat in the fire outside. Peter volunteered to do that as he was anxious to see if it was cooked. He used two flat rocks to roll it out of the fire onto an evergreen bough. He then dragged the bough into the cave. They just sat there exhausted but sort of gleeful in how they'd accomplished so much. The air filled with the flapping of wings and shrieking. Hundreds of bats came flying into the cave. They swarmed back into the cave amidst the screaming of Peter and Andy. What an experience that was for them. Peter and Andy put their hands over their heads to protect themselves. It took awhile before the bats became quiet as they settled into the ceiling farther down the cave. Both the boys sat there not being able to speak as they were breathless from seeing this.

Soon hunger set in with Peter and Andy opening the package of the baked rabbit meat. Since it was a small bunny, it should have cooked quickly, which it did. Carefully they each bit into a piece and relished the flavor. They let it cool and packed the rest back into the tin foil package for later use.

They decided they should sleep some more with each taking turns to stand rather sit guard at the opening of the cave. Peter suggested that Andy should sleep first. Andy chuckled as he said to Peter, "Look what happened last night when I went to sleep." Peter assured him that all would be quiet now. He was right. Taking turns sleeping gave them some much needed rest. It was just what they needed at this time. Then they took out some of the rabbit meat eating a minimal amount to keep the hunger at bay finishing with some berries for moisture. They took one last look outside of the cave entrance and knew that they needed to proceed into the cave to look for water. One last task was to find a small rock to write on the wall of the cave with an arrow pointing in the direction that they were proceeding into and their initials in case their dad or the Rangers located the cave. Hefting their packs on their backs, they took a deep breath of the cool air taking the first steps into a journey to a place they couldn't even imagine. Thinking ahead of what they might need, they decided to pull along the tree branches wrapped together by the rope and twine that they gathered the night before so they would be able to build a fire.

As they proceeded, it became dark. Turning on one of the flashlights intermittently to guide them, they would take a few steps staying close to the wall of the cave to feel their way. In addition, it was so quiet that they felt they had to whisper to each other. Both were comfortable with that as they didn't have much to say right now any way. The air was still fresh and cool as they proceeded which was comforting to them. Peter finally spoke saying, "Andy, I think we should make some marks on the wall of the cave so we can find our way back." Andy agreed and took out the small rock to make an arrow pointing in the direction they were walking. He made the arrow about chest high and large enough to see on the left side of the cave wall. The progress was slow but neither of them was in hurry. Now it was time to use caution with each step they took. Several hours later and several arrows on the wall, Andy asked them to stop and rest. Andy said he was hungry and could they eat a bit more. Peter was anxious to continue but respected Andy's request. He laid his backpack on the sand then asked Andy, "What would you like to eat?" Andy responded with the suggestion that they take a bit of the granola in a bag they had in their back pack. Peter thought that was a good idea pouring a bit for each of them as it was in his pack. Oh, it tasted good. They ate a few more berries for moisture while they sat and rested.

They stood up turning off the flashlight feeling their way along the wall while taking a few steps at a time. This process went on for most of the next few hours. One thing they did not forget was to make the marks on the wall though. This seemed so important to them. It was one more important lesson that they had learned since yesterday. As they walked along, they chuckled about Peter asking Andy what he wanted to eat and thankful that they had a choice now. They were careful in turning on the flashlight for a moment to look ahead then taking a few steps at a time. The air was still comfortable. It was dry in the cave which made breathing comfortable. They commented to each other that they would have supposed that it would smell musty. "Oh! Oh!" Andy said to Peter," something is changing in the way we are going. I feel the sand is different." They kept the flashlight on to check out what was happening and saw that there was a juncture ahead. It was lucky they saw it so they could decide which path to take. Andy wanted to stay on the path they were on. Peter did not. He said, "We should take the tunnel that leads downward so we can find water then we can return back the way we came."

Andy staunchly objected. He thought that it was not safe to go down. He said, "I am afraid of that tunnel as it may take us too low into the mountain. What if it rains which could bring torrents of water drowning us?" He went on relating about studying that in geography. Peter also recalled stories that he had heard about how the caves were formed with rivers running through them. He was adamant though. They talked about what if it rained hard then the forest fire would be doused by the rain allowing them to turn around to go back. Andy wouldn't budge so they just stood there. How to decide which way to go? As they had no one to help them to decide what to do they just waited for awhile.

The darkness was so stark. Nothing could have prepared them for this kind of darkness. With no stars, moon, sun, or clouds, it appeared as if they were in a void. Now they could feel what it was to be totally blind with no sight at all. Andy finally said he was going to sit down but then felt the sand was wet. He reached up to feel the walls of the cave. They were wet also. So wet that the rock would not leave a marker arrow on it. Panic set in with him. He said, "Peter, what should we do?" Peter answered that his instinct told him that they proceed downward very slowly. Andy finally agreed but left his flashlight on. As they started to walk, Andy admitted that he feared going any further down as there was the possibility that they could get lost and not find their way back. Peter agreed with that fear yet they couldn't just sit here. Besides that they couldn't go back without finding some fresh water. They slowly trudged on. They still made the direction marks on the wall even though they didn't make much of an impact. In addition, Andy now began to use his Swiss Army knife to make an X. He wanted to be sure that they could find the markers.

This tunnel finally opened up some and the walls were wet enough for them to lick some water off the wall. Oh, it tasted so fresh and clean. Peter wondered how much further they could go until they found a waterfall or stream. They kept Andy's flashlight on to see the way as they could make better progress that way which gave them confidence. Soon Andy again noted there was a change in the sand. He could feel it. Excitedly he said "Peter, we are slowly going up again." He felt the sand which wasn't as wet as before. He became hopeful that they were going up. With the few drops of water they got from the walls, it helped to refresh them. Soon Peter told Andy that he felt they were climbing some also. They still kept the flashlight on to see where they were going. They talked of finding some springs of some sort to fill the bottles with fresh water. They would even splash some on their heads and faces.

Since the sand was a bit drier, they decided to sit down to rest and to eat. They took out the berries and some of the nuts that they had gathered before they left the cave entrance. It gave them strength and more vigor. After the argument about whether to turn up or go down at the juncture, there had been discomfort but now that went away. They sat there now almost falling asleep. Some of the pressure to safeguard themselves lifted as they sat together.

The talk came back to the danger of storms with heavy rains that could flood the tunnels. "Since it was August," Peter said, "a storm could build bringing lightning and down bursts of rain. From what I know of years past though, it would be unusual. I remember practicing soccer most days without rain." Andy felt better about that. They sat in the dark to save the batteries of the flashlight. Not only was it dark, dark, it was also so quiet. They couldn't hear even a trickle of water. That worried them some. The quiet was so loud that it hurt their ears so they began to hum. After awhile, they wondered if some of the pressure on their ears was due to altitude. It was better after they hummed so they thought maybe it leveled off the pressure in their ears. They began to notice a change in the color of the cave walls as well. When they began the color was a deep, rusty brown. As they progressed, the color became lighter colored except where the walls were weeping water. This became a topic they discussed as they both felt it was due to water. Also they noted that the cave walls were darker close to the cave floor with a lighter color farther up. This became a concern as they wondered if they were now walking away from the water. So they took some time to assess their situation. Peter wondered out loud why the air was so fresh. Surely there must be an opening somewhere. Yet it wasn't really a breeze. Also why were the caves walls wet in some places and dry in others as well as the sand underfoot? He and Andy talked about this as they sat resting in the dark cave they were in.

One subject hung heavy in their minds. Finally, Peter asked Andy "I am wondering what is going on outside. Are there people out there looking for us? Mom and Dad must be in a panic wondering where we are." Andy was quiet for awhile, then adding that he really couldn't think of that as it was too much for him to imagine the pain that their mom and dad were going through. He said, "Let's just keep going and not talk about it for now."

Peter didn't feel ready to go yet. He asked Andy, "Do you think that we could be circling around in here? I know you have been putting arrows on the walls of the cave specifically on your left side for us to find on our way back. I haven't seen anything familiar yet we need to be aware of this. This is how we got in this jam in the first place by not paying close attention."

Andy replied that he agreed plus he had been etching the walls. He also told Peter that he did not want to go much faster as there could be the chance they would miss something. They both were doing well with the bit of water and the food so they talked for awhile yet.

Peter asked Andy what he thought he would like to be when he grew up Andy said, "You go first and I will think about it." Peter said he would like to be an astronaut. He shared that he liked more than the adventure of it. There were many books about the value of space travel. There were so many opportunities like the International Space Station. His hero is John Glenn who now is a supporter of the shuttles to the I. S.S. Who knows that maybe he could be involved with a station on the moon. You know I always liked Star Wars. Then my Science teacher, Mr. Beyer, took us on a field trip to the Science Museum. I learned so much there. There were displays of UFO's and aliens. It was so fascinating to see what they probably looked like. He added, "I could have stayed there for hours looking through the material and the displays. Soon you will go there, too. Sometimes I lie in bed at night looking at the moon thinking of what it would be to travel there or among the stars. Now how about you little brother? What interests you?" Peter seemed genuinely interested in what Andy would like to become. Andy took a deep breath then said that he would like to be a veterinarian as he liked taking care of animals especially horses and dogs.

After he had read about the herds of wild horses, he began to think about what it would be like to adopt one from the government. He said, "I checked out a book from the school library and read about them. I like animals in general though and I am sure that I could do that well. There are so many animals that need care."

This brought up the picture of their dog, Brownie, to Andy's mind. "Remember when we went to the Humane Society to pick up Brownie, our yellow lab, who turned out to be a great friend to us. There were so many animals there that needed care also." added Andy. Peter asked Andy "I wonder what would have happened if we had brought Brownie with us? Remember Dad thought he would run through the high grass and be a distraction."

Andy thought for while then said "Brownie would have helped us find our way home." Then they resumed the conversation about their futures. Both deep in thought about each other and what they had shared. At home there was so much going on, places to go and interruptions that they spent little time together talking about each other and their aspirations. It was a bond between them now. Peter told Andy that he was proud of what he had shared with him and he thought Andy would be a great animal care giver.

It was time to trudge ahead. So after Andy make another

arrow with the rock and mark with his knife, they turned on the flashlight and moved on. It was difficult to determine day or night where they were. Even looking at their watches, they couldn't determine the day from the night. They had been so involved in their activities since leaving the cave entrance that now it was either 3:30 in the afternoon or 3:30 in the early hours of dawn. Andy wondered to Peter, "Do you think we walked a whole day with the clock going past midnight into the next morning?"

Peter thought for awhile then responded that he couldn't tell either. He asked Andy if he was tired and wanted to sleep for awhile to which Andy responded that he thought they should go on for awhile yet. They kept the flashlight on now intermittently again feeling their way along the walls a few steps at a time, then turning on the light to mark the walls and look ahead. It seemed like the best plan for now. When Andy turned on the flashlight to look ahead and make another mark on the wall, he couldn't believe what he saw. There was a trickle of water running down the stone wall. He and Peter each took a sip. It tasted fresh and sweet. They opened their water bottles and the cup from the scout kit and filled them. Just to make sure though they threw a piece of aspirin in each bottle to purify it. It was decision time again. So they mulled over the advantages of going back or staying the course. The positives to go on were that the air was fresh, small amounts of water were available and they had sufficient supplies. Without any major setbacks, they could possibly find an exit on the other side of the mountain. While on the other hand, they could turn around following the marks on the walls to the cave entrance. They talked about the fire and not knowing what conditions were, they could possibly still be blocked in. Memories of the fire burned strong in their minds. So to lighten the mood, they tossed a coin with heads to go back. They threw the coin in the air with it coming up tails. Fate confirmed the decision to go ahead.

They were grateful that they had brought the boughs and sticks in addition to the scraps of cones, bark and sap pieces. It slowed them some dragging the material yet something like instinct told them to continue what was working for them. The routine of light on, light off strategy was also working for them. They felt safe in the knowledge that they could find their way back to the cave entrance if they found any kind of obstruction ahead as they had diligently marked the walls of the cave and reinforced the mark with a knife scratch.

So they walked on, chatting lightly about the surroundings and what they might see ahead, hoping it would be about the same with no surprises. The size of the cave walls did not change much which gave them plenty of head room.

As they walked on, Andy asked if soon they could stop for awhile to eat something as he needed a rest stop. Peter looked at his watch dial which read 6:00. Of course, not knowing 6:00 in the evening or 6:00 in the morning, he told Andy that it was probably good time for them to look at their supplies and eat what was still edible then takes turns getting some sleep as it seemed safe here.

Peter took his flashlight out of his backpack followed by his scout kit and the manual. He showed it to Andy saying it was full of projects and helpful information. He said that he now wished that he had studied it better especially the part of self help in case of emergencies. He then took some time to tell Andy about being a cub scout which traced back to the ancient Indians in this country. Many stories were told of how the Indians lived off the land in harmony with nature along with traditions of the tribes. The first badge is the bobcat followed by the wolf, bear, lion and then a scout at 12 years of age. The cub scouts learned to do things to improve their life as they begin to grow up.

He added, "You learn much about loyalty and listening to advice from the leader's experience. We learned how to make and find things. Other subjects to learn about were how to make knots in a rope, whittling, using tools, music, camping, cooking and how to be safe. It was a good training ground for the boy scouts. I will tell you more another time though."

So they went back to looking at what food they had and what they would choose for now. At least now they had some water. They wouldn't have to worry if it was safe either as the aspirin would do that for them. So they lunched then put their material back into the pack. Andy then laid down on his pack closing his eyes falling into a deep sleep. He dreamed that Peter was calling for him over and over again. Finally he jarred awake with the realization that it really was his brother calling to him but now in a weak voice. He struggled to wake up then crawled over to Peter who was burning up with a fever.

Alarmed, Andy asked him what was the matter. Peter whispered back that he was very ill and feeling faint. He said, "Listen carefully to what I am about to tell you. First give me a sip of water then I will tell you what to do." Andy reached for Peter's water bottle and held it to Peter's lips. He was shaking so badly fearful that he would spill some. He did alright with Peter slowly sipping the water. Peter put up his hand that he had enough for now.

Then he whispered that Andy should undo the rope that the twigs and branches were wrapped in, find the biggest one and stack the rest by the side for building a fire. He further instructed Andy to take out a sock and wrap it around the end of the chosen stick which he should stick into the ground. Then take out the tree sap wrapped in tin foil, rub some on a sock being careful on how much gets on his hand as it is really sticky, and then re-wrap the sap to keep it from getting sandy. Rub some sand on your hands to clean off the sap. Find a match, light it and then light up the sock end which has the sap on it.

He then said, "Andy, I feel weak and wonder if my temperature is high. I don't know what caused it but I was thinking it was either from cleaning the rabbit or from the bat droppings we walked through." He further told Andy that he must have been exposed to something. If it was the rabbit, he had learned that if there were red pimples on the belly, he could have been exposed to a bacterial virus which would cause a fever even though the rabbit looked healthy. He told him to get out the scout kit and boil the rabbit meat in a bit of water along with some of the roots they had gathered. It would be bitter but it was necessary to do this as they needed the broth.

Then he added that actually he thought it was more than likely his shoes picked up something from walking through the bat droppings or breathed in the micro spores carried in the air. There were so many bats that this was likely what happened. He would get a fever and he needed Andy to keep calm. He would get more ill but he would fight to get over it. He strongly urged Andy to get out the scout book and look for some remedies. He then dropped into a deep sleep. Andy felt an overwhelming panic. Here he was all alone in the dark with only a flashlight and a sick brother. He screamed out loud and then began to cry. As the tears rolled down his cheeks, he felt so sorry for himself. Out loud he asked, "Why me? How did this get me here? What am I to do?" The silence was deafening. There wasn't even an echo. He was resentful that he was left with the responsibility. He wanted to throw the rabbit meat out as he did not want to touch it. He could get sick also and then what. How come, he thought, did Peter get this fever from whatever and I didn't. We walked together and I am ok. He was startled by the next thought.

What if he got the fever also he questioned himself. They would die for sure here in this cave with no one knowing where they were. So he sat there mulling over situations in his head. Thoughts of home along with mom and dad flashed before him. Common sense began to take shape with him remembering what Peter had told him. The family was counting on him now.

He calmed down some now thinking of what he had to

do. He began to talk out loud to hear what he was saying as this helped him to organize his list of what he had to do. He wanted to leave the flashlight on to help settle his nerves and lessen the anxiety. He didn't though.

He heard Peter moaning over and over again then whispering mom, mom, and mom. For awhile he would be quiet then the moans would begin again with dad, grandpa, grandma. It was so quiet that Andy continued to talk out loud of what his thoughts were and began some action to help the situation. He heard Peter saying that he was so sorry followed by Andy help me. This jarred Andy into action.

He voiced what Peter had told him to do and begin the healing of his brother. First, he got out his sweatshirt, rolled Peter over on his side and laid the sweatshirt under Peter's back. His head was already on the back pack. Then he placed a cap on Peter's head. Somewhere he remembered that there is less heat loss. Even though Peter was in the throes of a high temp, he was probably cold also. He turned on the flashlight to get items out of his back pack that he would need. A pair of socks and matches for sure.

After he had retrieved what he needed out of his pack, he put it under Peter's head exchanging the two packs. He kept the flashlight on to see and to make sure he was doing these activities correctly. He did not want to lose something. Time wasted seemed like it would put Peter's life in jeopardy. From Peter's back pack he took what he would need then he rolled it under Peter's knees. Why he didn't know as it seemed like the right thing to do. He kept talking out loud which helped keep him calm.

He then wrapped one sock around the tip of one of the evergreen boughs after accessing the small packet with the tree sap in it. It gleamed in the light changing colors from a deep ruby to an amber color. He rubbed it thoroughly on the sock and then questioned himself if it would burn as he wanted it to. He envisioned a torch with a glow of light all the while thinking of how Peter had so carefully gathered the material from the crevasse not knowing how useful it would now be. As Andy was talking out loud he struck the match on the side of the box with a swift jerk lighting it. Slowly he moved it over the sappy sock. It tried to burn but it went out. He then knew he would have to shelter the flame with his free hand. He struck another match and it burned as it touched the gem colored sap. Slowly it came to life with a glow. Walla! It was working. What a win! Andy took a deep breath. Now he could turn off the flash light. He then put his efforts into starting a small fire to heat water with the scout pan.

He turned to Peter saying, "Good job in keeping this in

your backpack. I'll bet you thought it was not worth the weight but now it is just what we need." As he was getting set up, he talked out loud repeating the instructions that Peter had given him. Instead of picturing Peter lying there in the throes of the fever, it was just like he was sitting there telling him step by step what to do.

The glow of the sap burning on the sock was just enough to take off the stigma of darkness. Soon he would have a few boughs burning to heat the water to cook the rabbit meat and some water. After cooling it, he could make good use of the broth. With the use of the little spoon in the kit, he could drip some into Peter's mouth to stem off the parched throat. It would be necessary to keep a cool sock on Peter's head and then lift him as often as he could to drop a few drips of the broth into his mouth. He also got out a bandana to use if he needed it to cool Peter's body. Peter was not responsive to touch but Andy could feel the heat. He recalled that when his little sister had the measles and what his mother did to cool her off. He did not have a bathtub like at home but he could sponge Peter's body with the cool water and the sock while continuing the drip of broth.

He no longer suffered from remorse or self pity. He put all his effort into staving off the rising temperature in his brother's body which was more than likely from a virus of some sort from the bat droppings being the likely source. The fire would also help keep the temperature even for Peter. Andy kept the fire to the least he could just to keep it going. He used the antiseptic to clean his hands and ate some morsels of food to keep himself going as he dared not get drowsy or sleepy.

He also remembered that his mother had spoken that the temperature would be high for up to 24 hours before it would begin to wane. He began to plan on how to keep Peter dry when the sweat would begin about the time the temperature would peak. He could use his sweat shirt to put on Peter. As he was a bit smaller than Peter, his tee shirt would be too constricting to wear but it would be a good dabber. He would dry out the shirt that Peter was wearing and keep changing the shirts to keep Peter from being too wet. Andy munched some on the bit of granola and the berries that were left. He put some more roots in the pan to cook over the fire to feed to Peter. This went on for hours but Andy did not flinch once in his routine of cooling the sock on Peter's head and the dripping in the broth from the meat and the roots.

In a piece of tin foil, Andy found some orange colored stuff that looked like fungus that was attached to a piece of bark. Andy wondered if he heated it in a container with a bit of water then applied it like a compress to Peter's body perhaps it would help to pull out the infection causing the temperature. He didn't know so he did it anyway.

As he was doing his chores, Andy thought of why he had skipped being a cub scout. He was busy with other activities like bowling. Andy liked to read spending many hours with books. Now he wished he would have listened to his brother who had invited him to come to the meetings. He looked into the Boy Scout manual for more information that would be helpful in this situation. Looking at his watch, it was now midnight or was it noon. Actually it didn't matter except he wanted to keep time to see if his remedies were working.

This all seemed so turned around as it was usually Andy getting the attention and the care. Andy felt more grown up than he had ever felt.

DAY 3

Thursday August 14

PETER WAS NOW silent with no sound so Andy talked telling him stories from books he had read. His favorite series was the Hardy Boys. He related stories from them to pass the time as he gave Peter more broth and kept him cool. He talked on to keep himself and Peter entertained hoping that Peter could hear. The Hardy Boys named Frank and Joe were teenage brothers portrayed as amateur detectives. They were in the same grade in high school even though Frank was 16 and Joe was 15.

The cases were often linked to confidential cases that their detective father, Fenton, was involved in. Often times the father asked them for help as they could do some things he couldn't. In the stories, there were villains, adventure and action. The boys were never afraid of danger and took risks in seeking out the murderers, drug peddlers, diamond thieves and more exciting characters. Andy kept telling Peter about the stories while changing the cooling cloth and giving broth.

The fire was still going but only the embers. Andy guessed that Peter would now know what he was doing while Peter went to cub scouts and later on the boy scouts. He explained that he learned so much from reading books. One thing he remembered was to look abit to the left or right of an object in the dark as it became clearer. There are fewer sensor cells in the center of the eye. So by looking to the left of an object, there were more sensor cells in the surrounding eye making the object more visible. This went on for hours. Soon Andy looked at his watch and it was 8:00. The last time he had looked it was 12:00. There were still many hours to go but Peter didn't seem to be getting worse so Andy surmised that what he was doing was helping and he aimed to continue.

Andy kept up the vigil. He was cautious not to eat too much and to drink only minimally to ensure that the supplies would last until they found their way out of the cave back into the sunshine with clouds in the sky. Soon Andy realized that the rabbit meat was almost finished. He ate the last remains of it so as not to waste any morsel.

He dug out the venison jerky tearing off a small piece

putting it into the pan with the roots and the water. This time though he added a few small pieces of a tootsie roll candy. He put a few pieces of a bough on the embers to bring up the heat. He looked at the candy bar considering on eating the whole thing. He carefully put it back in the pack. He tasted the broth and found it was pretty good. Andy began dripping some into Peter's mouth without spilling any. This went on for at least another four hours. It was now 12:00 with Andy getting really tired. He took a sip of water. As he put the cap back on the bottle, Peter stirred. He was waking up some with moaning. Andy touched him to reassure him that he was there. Then he remembered how he used to like to sing. So he recalled all the songs he could and began to sing. This gave him some energy to continue. Several hours later he could only hum. Peter again stirred and mumbled that he was really thirsty. Andy immediately put the water bottle to his mouth and slowly dripped some in. Peter opened his eyes with a look of panic as to where he was and what had happened. Andy related about the temperature. He changed the sweatshirt on Peter and hung the other one on the boughs to dry. His tee shirt he used to dab the beads of sweat on Peter. By 6:00 Peter was fully awake and coherent. The temperature had dropped some leaving him with chills. Andy built up the fire by adding a few more pieces. He tore off a piece of jerky for Peter to suck on giving himself a chunk also.

He told Peter that he needed to get a few minutes of shut eye and that Peter should be sure to call him if he slept too long. Peter nodded still weak but alert. Andy lay down on the sand falling asleep. He dreamed that he was at home with his mom rubbing his back and humming to him. For awhile this comforted him. He awoke with a start remembering where he was. Peter was awake asking for more to drink and eat. This, in Andy's estimation, was a good sign. He prepared some more broth then helped Peter to sip it. They were going to be ok. After both of them felt refreshed, Andy helped Peter to get up to do some personal relief. They lay around most of the next few hours.

Finally, Andy stated that he was going to pack things up as it was time to move on. He fashioned a traverse for Peter to use intermittently as he was so weak. Andy used the ropes to tie some boughs together to use as as traverse. He helped Peter get aboard, laid Peter's pack toward the top then strapped his pack on. Then they set off to go deeper into the cave. Soon Peter became strong enough to walk on his own.

The air had more movement which made the boys wonder what was ahead. They came upon a chamber that filled them with amazement and awe. The chamber opened into a large room that was cool but dry. The walls seemed to be limestone rock with water dripping off the ceiling forming small streams flowing into larger pools. There was water cascading down large layers of rock tilting upwards sliding over other layers.

Looking around some more, they saw stalactites forming columns from the top of the cave ceiling towards the floor along with many stalagmites forming from the floor upward which appeared to be mineral formations. Everywhere there were springs flowing from the rock layers. The colors were spectacular from the rock layers to the cave walls with an overall greenish glow. To Peter and Andy, they reached a utopia. All they could think about was cavorting in the streams, drinking all the water they wanted and splashing around in it. They took off their clothes to jump into a pool. It was warm and felt like mineral water. As they were low on energy and strength, they laid in the water letting it flow over their bodies that had survived a forest fire, long days of trudging in the dark, bats, illness and lack of water. They just lay there letting it all flow away from them. Soon they washed their clothes and hung them to dry on the rocks. Since they were alone, they did not worry that they were without their clothes on. The clothes really needed to be

washed as they smelled badly. Not really knowing how many days had transpired since they had showered the morning they had left home, they now felt cleansed.

They preserved the precious pieces of tree boughs that they had dragged along. Then they found some morsels of food and lay down to relish this strange, almost eerie place inside of a mountain. They agreed that no one would ever believe this place existed then dozed off to sleep.

DAY 4

Friday August 15

ON WAKING, THEY felt so refreshed yet famished. They needed to find more food even though they had venison jerky left. While chewing little bits of this, they looked around to see what they could use.

Andy, walking barefoot, went further than Peter who was still weak. He looked in the pools for fish. He did find some small ones while wondering just how to snag them as they didn't have a net or a hook. Going back to Peter, he sat down beside him to talk about what he had found. There was plenty of moss along with the tiny fish. He asked Peter, "Would you have any idea on how to catch the fish?" Peter responded that he would have to think on this.

In the meanwhile, he asked Andy to fill him in on what transpired while he was ill. Andy did his best to tell him how he had instructed Andy on what to do, what to use and how to do it. He used most of the sap on the sock, the fungus for a compress, the broth with the rabbit meat and roots cooked together plus at the end some jerky. He asked Peter if he could remember anything at all.

At first Peter said no but then faintly recalled stories and singing. Peter told Andy that it was like a dream seeing his mom, dad and grandpa yet knowing they were not here. He had strange visions of being somewhere hearing a voice singing. He asked Andy, "Was that you singing to me?

I never heard that before. I am learning more and more about you, little brother." Besides that he added I now realize that you saved my life. He went on to say that together they experienced situations that he felt would bond them for life. Andy responded that at first he got a panicky feeling being isolated and alone. Then it seemed as if Peter had been there talking him through what needed to be done. He had to think of ways to stay awake to tend Peter and the little fire needed to heat water so he thought of stories then singing to while away the hours. He said as the hours moved on, he had a positive feeling that Peter would mend quickly. He reached over and held up his hand to do a high five.

They sat quiet for some time before making some decisions regarding the availability of food sources. They both agreed that they should stay here for awhile to recuperate. They worried that the days were slipping by with their parents searching for them. Still they needed this respite and who could have asked to be in such an idyllic place, like an oasis in a desert.

Andy asked Peter if he had his watch which he had left with the back pack before he fell asleep. Peter said no he hadn't but they would look for it after awhile. It was a curious thing.

First they needed to inventory what food was left. At least the worry of water was gone for now. They opened their packs and began to see the meager bits left. They still had the candy bar, small pieces of granola mostly oatmeal, some tootsie rolls, pine cones, the dried flower from the crevasse, several pieces of jerky, a little piece of tree bark, some pine nuts and that was about it.

Until they could assess what was edible in this ideal place, they would need to depend on the jerky. They mulled over making a broth with the dried flower with a bit of tree bark which could be made tastier with a piece of tootsie roll. So they took a small branch cutting it into small pieces, set a match to light it. After the mixture cooled they tasted it with a smile saying that was pretty good. They finished it off by chewing on another piece of jerky. Peter was really exhausted laying down on the sand with his pack under his head ready to fall asleep when Andy was puzzling to where his watch was. It was not in the items they had just looked at. He told Peter that he was going to look at the area where they had washed their jeans. He was also going to look for some quick things to eat. Oh how he missed the berries. Just the memory of them made his mouth water. Peter was sleeping as Andy walked off.

He searched high and low for the watch in the green light then decided he needed to use his flashlight. It was all for naught as the watch was gone.

He gave up for now knowing that he had to find some things for them to eat. There didn't appear to be any grass or green bushes. If they didn't find anything soon, they would have to move on. They did not want to lose the strength they had just recouped. There was plenty of moss so he wondered what to do with it. He went back to talk it over with Peter when he spotted a small frog. Wow! He thought that would make a good soup. Peter was still sleeping soundly so Andy searched his mind to try to remember some things he had read about caves, plants, animals and insects. He had a series of books he had read some while back. He wondered if they could locate some algae. He didn't seem to be able to concentrate as his mind was befuddled to what happened to his watch. It was precious to him as it had been a gift from his mom and dad. It had a leather strap with a clasp so it couldn't have slipped off. He would have felt that. He didn't like this feeling of not paying attention to something that meant so much to him. He was certain that he had laid it on his backpack before going to sleep.

Peter stirred then sat up rubbing his eyes saying he felt so rested. Andy told him about the moss and the frog. Peter was excited about this yet he thought of how that frog got here. He began to wonder if it came with a flash flood. Surely there wasn't enough here to sustain frogs. Peter suggested that they should talk out loud about anything that came to their mind about caves, plants and animals. Andy agreed by taking the first shot. He said he recalled from some books he had read about spelunker reports on what they observed. Starting with the fungus on the walls of the cave, it could be converted to food. Moss could be cooked as a soup or porridge. These were all sources of food. He had read about lichen which is organisms which can survive in extreme conditions as the arctic where reindeer eat it. Except he remembered that when working with it, purple bumps can be a result which is itchy to the skin. Lichen though is low in protein and high in carbs, still that may work for us.

"Whew!" said Peter "where did you get all this information?" Andy replied that he read magazines and books on this. He added that while you were so ill, I had to remember what you told me you had learned and I thought I should have done that also. Then I thought of all the books I've read. I have learned so much from them. "This is good" said Peter "We are making a great team". He asked Andy if he saw any algae but thought that algae needed sunlight so it wouldn't grow in a cave. Then they talked again about how that frog got here. Andy laughed as he said, "The frog probably came the same way we did, by accident." Peter kind of agreed. If that was so, they could probably catch it and make stew or something with it. Yet if not, he didn't want to upset nature.

So Peter shared that they should look for those fish that Andy had found and see if maybe there were any other things they could catch. They needed food but did not want to disturb the balance going on in the cave. He said he felt stronger and could manage to walk around some. Some fish could even make him stronger. They went to check out the pool where Andy had seen them.

On the way, they looked with beady eyes to observe what else there was. As they walked, they talked about the green light which was not natural. It was all around them but they wondered where it was coming from. Soon they arrived at the fish pool. There were gobs of tiny fish. They wondered what the fish were eating as there didn't seem to be any source of food for them.

Andy asked "Do you think that once in awhile, there is a rush of water that could bring in ants, bugs, algae or something else they eat?" Peter shrugged his shoulders as he was not at all familiar with any of this. They looked the situation over and then wondered how to catch enough for them to cook. Peter hit upon an idea. They could use the strainer part of his Boy Scout kit and catch them that way. They could run that through the water and scoop them up.

Peter related that the scout master had found these strainers that clipped to the cooking kit and offered them to his scouts. The scout master had told them it would be a good item to have in case there was debris in the water, the strainer would be perfect to sort that out.

Then Andy added he could scrape off some moss from the rocks then they could make a fish stew. They were already hungry and could almost smell the dish. So they set about with this project. It gave them a surge of energy as they worked together. Andy broke up a few pieces of the evergreen boughs to make a fire while Peter sorted out the fish to cook. Then Andy went to get some moss off the rocks with his knife. While it was cooking, the boys talked about how strange these fish looked. They were pale almost white and some appeared not to have any eyes either. This didn't matter to Peter and Andy as they were interested in the nutrition they would get. This was so exciting for them now to have water and fish. Soon they could eat and not worry about upsetting their digestive systems. They really needed some green stuff.

When they had finished their fine meal, they both chuckled. If they were at home with mom serving this they would say Yech! I won't eat that. There is no table here to set, no dishes to wash and very little cleanup. We wash our hands in the water and use sand to clean the pans and our knives. "Ok now," Peter said, "where is the dessert?"

Andy remembered to tell Peter that he had not located his watch. Peter wasn't as worried about it as Andy was. Where was it or what had happened to it. He said he had laid it on the back pack before they went to sleep and upon waking up, it was gone. He wondered if there was an animal in the area that would have been attracted to the shiny object. Peter pshawed the notion as he said they would have seen it by now. Before they settled in for the night, Andy asked if Peter thought there could be spiders in this cave. Up to now they hadn't seen any in the cave but, of course, this was the first place with an abundance of water.

Andy suggested they keep their guard up though both for sneaky animals and spiders. He also added that their sister,

Abby, and cousin, Allie, would shriek if they saw a spider. They laid down falling asleep and slept for a long time.

Peter was the first to waken and shook Andy. He was hungry again and was thinking of the frog. What should they do about it? They needed to have some protein before setting out to find a way out of the cave and needed something to take along to eat. If only they could find some more food. He thought that if there were any ants that came in, maybe there would be a lizard or a turtle. Now that would be enough to keep them going for several days to get out of the cave on the other side. The other side he mused to himself and wondered if there was a way or would they have to go back the way they came. He said to himself that if it was up to him he would go on. Yet Andy had a say in this also. For now though it was all about the search for food.

So they took a deep drink of the water that tasted so good. They had the feeling that they were being watched though. That was the first inkling of danger or wariness they'd experienced since arriving to the pool area. They looked under the rocks and found some small, white objects that looked like shrimp. There were a jillion of them to eat. Protein would be what they'd get when they eat these. They could be cooked along with the blind fish they found yesterday. They scooped up a bunch of them then went to do the same with the fish. They would eat hardy today.

This would be good while they would be here but nothing they found yet would be good for transporting with them. They decided to catch the frog and cook it. It meant their lives so it was not too hard to decide. The frog could last for at least a day. They would try to catch it today and start on their way. Perhaps as they went they could probably locate other sources but remembering how barren the cave had been this far, there didn't seem to be much potential. The other thing they could look for was a turtle. Peter thought that he could shoot it with his pellet rifle. It seemed that it would be ok to shoot it in the cavern. Andy said that there were ants so perhaps there was a turtle or a lizard. They were going to search carefully. There did seem to be something else in this cave yet made itself scarce to them.

Peter wasn't frightened but now that he had regained his strength also his alertness came back. The fatigue and the lethargic feelings were gone now. He would always wonder what had triggered the illness that had besieged him. For now though, he was thankful that he was alive and able to continue his pursuit to safely bring his brother and himself back to the family. Other than that all else had to be set aside in his mind. He told Andy what he thought about catching the frog plus Andy's idea of looking for a turtle or lizard of some sort. Adding also that either could survive in the cave as there was adequate water and food. They joined forces to catch the frog which they knew would not be an easy target. Frogs were elusive at best. Andy said that he thought that the frog could be a robber type frog which lives in limestone caves or wet crevasses. He added though that there are so many species in the frog world.

They took their back packs along with them as they went hunting just to be sure that nothing more would go missing. They did leave their shoes behind and walked barefoot for now. The shoes were not dry yet from cleaning them from the long trek to get here especially Peter's pair that he had used some antiseptic hand cleaner on them to be sure that the virus was gone. So they tied a small rock to each shoe to secure them. If they ran into some sharp objects they could easily return to the site to get them. They were not going far. The air in this area was sort of dry not the damp conditions they had experienced in some places so far.

As they traversed a pool of shallow water, they saw lots more tiny fish which they could use again later on. For now they had to concentrate on the frog. It seemed to be gone or well hidden. They jumped some more small pools spending time to search each area for the frog. It seemed to have disappeared.

It was a disappointment to them as they decided to slowly walk back to the site where they had left their shoes talking about coming back later on. For now they had to catch some more fish and the little shrimp like creatures for a meal as they were hungry. It took awhile to get enough to feed two hungry boys who seemed to be enjoying themselves in spite of the disappointment in not finding the frog. They knew they had to cook a great number of the fish to last for hours as the supply of fire wood was also limited. They were fortunate in the temperature of the cave to keep them feeling dry and comfortable. Andy splashed some water on Peter just for fun. They cavorted around getting their shirts wet laughing and joking the whole time.

Upon returning to the site, the shoes were still there so they relaxed. Andy said, "I was not sure the shoes would be here then what would we have done. Instead of looking for the frog, we would have to find our shoes." They built a small fire and put the fish water on to boil. Again Andy scrapped off some moss to add to the soup. He was getting better at this. To make it taste better, they put a tootsie roll into the water, moss and fish. They chuckled about sweetening the pot. They sat down to drink the soup they had made and laid down on their packs to rest some. Peter and Andy began discussing that this was a setback as they would have to stay to find something more substantial to take along on the way ahead. Andy suggested that perhaps they should go back the way they came but Peter announced that he would like to push ahead to find a way out. For now, they just made small talk as Peter almost fell asleep again. Andy looked at his shoes then yelled, "My watch is here in my shoe. How could this be?" Peter became wide awake as he said back, "Andy, I am happy that your watch is back but now we know for sure there is something else in this cave. I am leery about this so we will need to take turns sleeping and guarding again. I don't think it is dangerous else why the watch would have been returned. It is like a trick. I am glad that I have my pellet rifle handy to use."

Now they were uneasy and wary of what was going on. Peter who was exhausted asked Andy to watch while he slept for awhile but to awaken him quickly if he spotted anything. Andy agreed.

He took Peter's Boy Scout manual to look through. There was plenty of light to read by even though the light was greenish. He looked up and around at the cave walls and sides wondering at the beauty of it all. How had all this been formed he asked himself. How could water do this? Then looking over at the cascading falls he knew that he would always remember this place as a refuge in spite of the unease about the watch. The colors would change at the waterfall causing a rainbow effect. He could have stared at it for hours on end. He picked up his watch to see if it was working or had been tampered with. It was ticking and there was no evidence of teeth marks on it from an animal. The strap did not have any marks on it either. This was strange he pondered for awhile on what had taken the watch then returned it. Again the uneasy feeling of being watched hit him. He quickly looked up and around without seeing anything. He inspected the area seeing no tracks of any sort now really became bewildered. Peter slept for awhile. Upon waking, he asked if Andy wanted to sleep. He was wide awake and suggested they look around. For the next while, they went to study the stalactites and the stalagmites. They were amazed at the height and span of them. Looking from the top down on the stalactites, it must have taken eons to form these structures. Then looking from the bottom up on the stalagmites was awesome. These formations would be imprinted in their minds forever. The colors were varied and seemed to change as the drips came down the stalactites. They walked around them and felt them as they resembled huge icicles. It was something they had never imagined could be possible. The stalagmites resembled mineral deposits and were too big to put their arms around them.

It was slippery and wet so they decided to just look at them from the distance. Back in school, they would remember this part of the adventure as they had learned so much. They sat down at the base to take it in all the while chewing on a piece of jerky. They both enjoyed the taste. Andy and Peter commented that they had each lost some weight but were feeling good.

By now, Andy was thinking he was getting tired asking Peter to take up guard while he slept. Peter agreed and lay down on his back looking around the cave to remember all of this humming a bit while Andy fell into a deep sleep. Andy dreamed that the cave turned dark; the green light gone. He awoke with a start asking Peter if all was okay. The greenish light was still there but Andy wondered if the dream had been an omen.

DAY 5

Saturday August 16

SOON HE THOUGHT they would find the frog, cook some stew and move ahead or back the way they had come. He had a premonition that saddened him. He suggested to Peter that since they had both slept they could go look for the frog to which Peter agreed. They hefted the packs on their backs, tied their shoes to the bag and walked among the pools. This time they were going to be successful. Peter took out his Boy Scout kit in case they needed it with the search now on. They quietly lay by a pool where Andy had spotted the frog and sure enough there it was. They put together a plan with Andy on one side and Peter on the other. Andy was to chase it to Peter who would clap the pan part of his kit on top of it. The wary little frog tried to escape as the pan came

down on top of it. Now it was trapped in the sand and this was going to be tricky.

Andy helped mound the sand up around it making a hill then slid the other part of the pan under it. It worked. They now had captured the frog. It wasn't big but with the fish, some moss, and the shrimp like creatures, they could cook enough broth to get them started. They still had the candy bar, tootsie rolls and some jerky so they knew that would be enough to survive. They returned to where the boughs were stacked and looked at the meager pile. It was hardly enough to cook the stew. It had to do though as that was all they had. It was sort of tricky to hold onto the frog so they gave it a knock on the noggin to stun it enough to clean it.

Andy started the fire and congratulated himself on this as he was getting good at it. Peter put together the works. Then they sat watching the last of the wood burning even using some of the pine cones they had in reserve.

Finally they could tell it was ready to eat. Just the aroma filling the area made them even hungrier. Peter said,"When we get back home, I am going to have a big burger with pickles and catsup." Andy agreed. They only drank the juice saving the solids for the journey which was soon to begin hopefully to find an exit out of the mountain. As they finished, Andy and Peter turned to look around as they had a strange sensation. There before them stood two rather large creatures that looked like aliens from outer space. They were about 4 feet tall; each had a bulging, huge eye in the middle of the forehead. They had no ears or nose but a small opening that could be called a mouth and a long tail. They were colored red and looked so frightening. Actually they looked much like a gecko. Their fingers were webbed. The boys were stunned and afraid. The aliens also acted afraid. Finally Peter muttered "Who, who are you and what do you want?" The aliens stared at them looking into Peter's eyes. Peter stood very still and then put up his hand. He looked over at Andy saying "They can read my mind. Try looking at that eye. Then think of what are they doing here." Andy stood real still and looked at the one eye of one of the creature. The eye of the alien turned iridescent and bright as the blood flashlight. It was like he went into a trance. He sensed that the alien could read what he was thinking. He wondered how the creatures could communicate back though. That was going to be a whole different matter. They looked at each other for a while then the aliens transported themselves away. Peter and Andy stared at where the aliens had stood. There were no footprints. This was eerie. Peter said to Andy, "I don't think they are mean or harmful. I am going to think on this for awhile."

Andy let out a deep breath as he thought it was eerie also. Peter lay down with his head on his pack then putting his arms behind his head began to think. He mulled all this over in his mind. He questioned all the aspects wondering how to talk to the aliens. He was so curious wondering how long they had been here, where did they come from and why did they come to earth in the first place. He fell asleep in this position. In a dream, he was in a spaceship cruising aimlessly among the stars. He dreamed that he saw other planets all of them devoid of life as people on earth defined life. Before he woke up, he pictured coming back to earth where the sky was blue with white clouds, oceans, green areas and mountains standing stately above the flat land. As he slowly woke up, he looked around here. It was almost like an anomaly as he and Andy had walked through a dark cave to come upon this idyllic place with all its beauty so it must have been for the aliens to find earth. Overall they must have had a purpose to come here. Was it to invade or to find something on this lush, green planet? He would have to find a way to hear their story. He looked around for Andy and found him fetching fish, moss and shrimpy creatures to cook. Andy had been as hungry as a bear. Andy brought the catch back to get help from Peter who was thankful for his brother's foresight as he was so hungry also. He could have eaten all of it raw.

He wondered what they would use for fuel to cook the fish. Andy had found an old piece of wood that must have been washed in. He said they could start with the pine cones then put this piece of wood on the fire. Good idea as far as Peter was concerned. He had a good sleep and now was refreshed. As they worked together he talked and talked to Andy about what he had dreamed about. Andy was amazed as this could be so. After they ate, they cleaned up their hands.

Peter then asked Andy if he remembered about a year ago, they had gone to the home of a "ham" radio operator for Boy Scout Jamboree on the Air. Andy shook his head in response as Peter went on. Amateur Radio Operators talk to other radio operators around the world with the universally excepted code to overcome the language barriers in the world. This radio operator, NOFBA, along with his wife, sons and a spouse all studied to become FCC licensed. They can either use the code or voice to talk around the world with their radio equipment. Then once a year, they invite boy scouts to their radio shacks to observe and participate hoping to create interest in ham radio. Remember how we kept on practicing the letters and numbers for awhile. He asked Andy, "Do you think you could remember some of them?" Andy said he could as it was of interest to him especially the letters but it would take some practice.

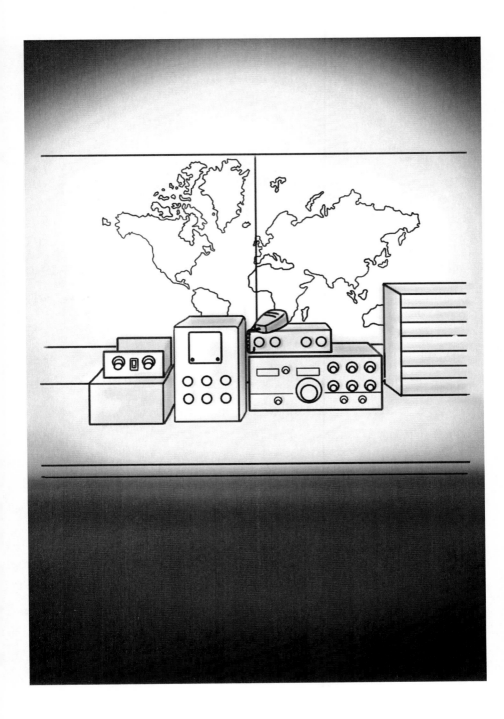

He asked Peter,"Why?" Peter said if they could put together a message in code perhaps they could talk to the aliens with it. Andy thought some then suggesting they could use the flashlight to blink it off and on to match the dits and dahs. It would take some real effort and practice but it just might work. So they began, staying with it for hours. Soon they were so tired that they laid their heads on their packs and fell asleep which lasted for hours. When they awoke, they were amazed at how well they could blink the light off and on. It was if they had been practicing in their sleep. Now they wondered how they would find the aliens questioning where they were. They ate some granola along with fresh water then went in pursuit of the aliens taking their backpacks with flashlights in hand. They climbed to the other side of the cavern leaving this ideal place behind. They knew they could always come back this way yet as they stood looking back they both sensed it would be their last look. Perhaps they wondered also if they could find out where the greenish light came from.

They were careful as the area they were walking in was wet and slippery making progress slow. Andy began to make marks on the wall again so they could find their way back if need be. Excitement built as they progressed along.

It didn't take very long when there it was, the spaceship.

It was silver colored, in the shape of a disk, had a smaller cap like dome on the top with a larger cylinder like bottom. It blinked as it sat there emitting a greenish glow. Andy and Peter looked at each in amazement as there was the green glow they had experienced in the cavern. Here was a space ship better known as a UFO right before their eyes.

It wasn't as big as they would have imagined but large enough carrying many objects. Large as it was looming before them, it didn't appear as an imminent danger to them. They were mesmerized by the object with a feeling of being frozen in your tracks. Peter remembered how he used to lie in his bed imagining being in such a craft zipping around among the stars now here was one right before his eyes.

Peter and Andy sat down on the sand to take all this in with neither saying a word. They stared at the dome at the top which had small cutouts that probably could have been windows or peep holes. It hummed in a quiet tone. Andy asked Peter,"What would be running in that quiet tone?" Peter thought for awhile then answered that he thought it could be like a generator. That seemed a likely possibility. They took out a piece of Jerky to chew on as they sat there watching the ship.

Soon the two aliens appeared before them silently standing there. Peter put up his hand with a friendly gesture thinking of greeting them while telling Andy to do the same. They held up the flashlights turning them on so the light shone up into the cave telling the aliens not to be frightened by them. They turned them off and on several times then handed them to the aliens telling them in their minds what they had said in flashlight code.

Peter thought in his mind that this would be a way for them to talk to each other. Soon the aliens handed them back. Andy took his then again began the dits and dahs by turning the flashlight off and on to match the letters in the words. The aliens comprehended what was happening by holding out their hands to take the flashlight back. Out loud Andy asked them about their ship. One alien blinked the light off and on with the answer. It was working. Yahoo! The brothers figured out the question in their head with aliens answering them with the blinking flashlights in code. It took awhile to synchronize the letters. The aliens were quick to learn nodding their heads. They told the brothers that they were from a planet located at the far end of the solar system. It was many light years away.

Since their home planet had its circular orbit around the sun altered, the conditions changed causing ice and cold.

Most of the citizens were wasting away from starvation. It was the dream of the elite that they continue their existence by all means including leaving their home planet. Therefore, the selection process was to have the strongest, the most intelligent and the healthiest citizens chosen to search the solar system for a new home that had sufficient sun which produces the photosynthesis for green plants. The space ship was specially designed with very superior technology for them to travel among the stars and the planets searching for the ideal conditions for them to take over the new place to expand their citizenry and to fulfill the mission they were committed to. The mission was to take over the military installations, disable power grids, eradicate radar systems, jam microwave signals and cause disruption to all forms of communication. Force was necessary. Earth was a good target as there were new sources of food available. It had the minerals, the water, the sunshine and all the necessary resources to sustain their life. Peter interrupted the story by asking them a question in his mind and out loud so Andy could hear. He asked, "If you had force as your mission, weren't you taking a chance that your space ship could be destroyed along with the subjects like yourselves?" They answered with the flashlight code that they thought their superior equipment and knowledge would easily conquer the civilization giving them freedom to rule the land as they had done on their planet. They went on to say that they were six feet tall when they began their journey believing that they had sufficient protein to sustain themselves. They believed they were stronger than they actually were and underestimated the combat force that they faced. They had to choose to run for it or be eradicated. Therefore, they used their lasers to cut a swath into this mountain thus lodging their vehicle into the earth. Chaos took over among them. Each of them was so strong and would not compromise in making decisions. It was different here as they were all equal with no class distinctions. The peaceful place that they had come from had not prepared them for the force they met up with. Many of them withered and dried up. Look at us, we shrank to the size we are today. They admitted that they had a flawed mission. Now all they wanted was to free their ship and go back into outer space. They said they were tired and almost out of propellant for their ship. Then they asked in code what the boys were doing here. Since they looked to Peter, he took the initiative to answer. He told them they also set out on an expedition that failed. There was a big fire that forced them into the cave to save their lives. They were looking for a way to get to the other side of this mountain to get out and then to go home. Peter said all this out loud even though the aliens could read his mind as he wanted Andy to hear what he had said. He also added that for both him and his brother this expedition was a lesson about survival and about brotherhood. Andy nodded. He said out loud that perhaps they could help each other get out of the mountain then they could all go home. The aliens asked them what they used for food. Andy answered now saying that they had gathered berries and pine nuts. Peter here used his pellet gun to get us a rabbit which we used. Also we brought a few things from home to get us through. Then when they came to the cavern, there were fish and shrimp creatures along with some moss on the cave walls. He looked at them asking what had they used the while they were marooned here.

Peter also said that was a good question. The one alien using the flashlight coded out that they were able to grow the organism called lichen.

He went on to say that each lichen consists of an alga and a fungus that live together in a plant partnership. The green alga produces food. The fungus absorbs water which is stored and captures mineral nutrients. Lichen does not require soil for growth. All algae contain the green pigment called chlorophyll. They manufacture sugar by a process called photosynthesis with the aid of the energy from the sun. The only draw-back is that it is low in protein and high in carbs. Since this was our only source of food, we have shrunk to half our size as I said earlier. It took a long time to set the correct amount of light the simple plants needed.

"Oh" answered Andy, "is that the green light that we see?" The aliens nodded in affirmation. The one alien went on to explain that they have perfected the process and could continue to sustain themselves. The realization became apparent to not only the aliens but also to Peter and Andy that they had learned to adapt to whatever it took to survive.

Also through this sharing, they learned that though they were from different worlds, they had a common goal which was that they wanted to go home. For Peter and Andy, this goal was easier as they had a home with a family nearby while the aliens wondered if they had a home to go to. Peter thought plus speaking out loud, "What would it take to free your ship from the mountain? We would be willing to help you as at the same time you would be helping us get out of the mountain." The alien responded that it would take some mental preparation. We are both resourceful and we have observed that you both are also. Here is how our ship works. Come aboard to see what how it works and then we will survey what is needed outside. There are many roots, vines and shrubs that have grown since we landed here. Those would need to be pulled apart. We are not physical creatures so that has kept us locked up here. Andy and Peter looked at each other with a nod thinking this would be a good job for us. They both had the same thought that their parents would not have believed this if they were here. They pouted and grumbled about helping pull weeds in the vegetable garden at home.

Andy said, "I want to ask you if it was you two who took my watch and then returned it in perfect shape?" They coded back that it was them investigating what it was.

The excitement was building with Peter and Andy hardly able to contain them with the thought that they were going to go aboard a UFO. They looked at each other unable to speak and could hardly breathe. Yes, yes, each one thought as the aliens led them to the ship. Automatically, the boarding plank lowered as if it knew they were ready to walk up and into the dream of any young man. The aliens led the way inside where the whole atmosphere was filled with the greenish glow. Neither Peter nor Andy showed any fear of entering as a trust had been established between them with the identification of a common goal which was to get out of the mountain. As they looked around, it appeared that they were in the disk part of the ship. There were many long tubes that the aliens told them were the restoration slots with one for each of them. Now you can see how many of us there were when we arrived. As our brethren withered away, we used their cubicles to grow lichen. It took some ingenuity to adapt the cubicles for food chambers but it was necessary to grow our favored food source. We perfected the process and now are ready to set out on the journey back to our planet knowing that we have the methods to save our people if there are any remaining.

Sure enough Peter and Andy saw all the tubes filled with material except for two chambers. Staring at the set up, Peter and Andy were fascinated. They also got hungry just looking at the food available. There was too much to look at and study so the thought of food was soon forgotten. They felt naive as they looked at how intelligent species could use their minds to the optimum to develop this method of survival. The way the green algae grew under the green lights that imitated sunlight was phenomenal. There was a platform to access the dome part of the ship where the mechanisms and flight equipment were located.

Peter and Andy followed the two aliens toward the conning tower filled with blinking lights, knobs, instrument panels, shift sticks, panels and touch screens. There were two pilot seats that could access the instrument panels and the touch screens from either one of them. Most of the equipment was compactly installed. They were able to look out of the cut outs that looked like windows which they had observed on the space ship from afar. The aliens explained that there are metallurgic shields that could be closed to protect the panels which would avert rocks in outer space or thwart off flying objects.

The space ship can rest in space with thrusters which are small propulsive devices for station keeping and attitude control in the reactive control systems. Out in space there is nothing to stop an object. It would go on forever as there is no opposing force to go against or grab it. By aiming the thruster in the opposite direction, there is something to create an opposing force. It can't be seen but the opposing force is there.

The aliens explained that their engineers chose tanks of extremely compressed air which when releasing the jets of air they push against the ground with the thrusters. The space ship forces air out of a series of nozzles. Since the compressed air is heavier, that push will have an opposing effect on the object being pushed. To simplify this they said an example would be to open the nozzle of a garden water hose. As the water comes out through the hose, it forces the hose to jump around. By grabbing the hold of the hose and holding it tightly, the spray can be directed. So it is with the space ship by starting the thrusters to accelerate, the force pushes the spaceship to overcome the gravity of earth.

The space ship uses propellant like fuel used in a rocket engine to gain speed and height. The outer shell is titanium with a nickel covering which is a hard metallic element that is resistant to rusting. The nickel was highly polished to make it shiny and smooth.

Once freed from the earth, we would need to quickly accelerate to avert the beams from the military monitoring systems that would direct F-18's to destroy our ship. The alignment of the planets is in close proximity now for us to take off and set in the direction of our home planet within the next two days. Otherwise we would have to wait until this occurs again. The offer to assist us in removing the plants and vines would be a benefit to us as our thin covering would burn off from the bright sun's rays. Your planet earth helped us to develop what we needed through the use of the natural resources and now we are ready to go.

DAY 6

Sunday August 17

ANDY AND PETER expressed that this tour was a dream of a lifetime but as young boys we now need to eat as we are so hungry. When we get this hungry, we are not able to absorb much information.

We cooked a frog before we left the cavern where we first observed you two. Then we drank the broth saving some of the meat to eat to give us strength. Please excuse us so we can get out our meal from our backpacks. The aliens nodded at each other as the boys each took a pan from the Boy Scout kit and put some food into it. They talked to each other agreeing that they would have to eat whatever they had cold as there were no supplies to build a fire with.

The aliens stood by them then reached out to take the boy's pans. They took them to the chamber where the tubes were located. Gently filling them, they carried them back to the boys who observed that they were now full. They began to sip what was in the pans smiling. The taste was fantastic with the contents smooth like a custard pudding. They sipped each drop feeling like they had drunk an elixir or an energy drink. An energy drink would never measure up to the flavor they had just savored.

Peter said to Andy, "This really tastes good and I feel so strong. Is it just me or do you feel the same way?" Andy shook his head at the same time responding that he had never tasted anything this good. They looked over at the aliens in gratitude saying they were ready to begin clearing the debris from the outside of the space ship. Using their hands to pull some vines and cutting some small branches with their Swiss Army knives, they diligently worked several hours.

They had both exerted a huge amount of energy but they did not feel tired. Soon they could see the other side of the space ship. The aliens were watching closely expressing admiration to what they now saw was the atmosphere.

They closed the tubes with the lichen. Then, they expeditiously fastened everything down to ensure that there would be no flying objects. Now the rest of the departure was up to them.

They turned on the ignitions to get the jet's thrusters

going. Peter and Andy stood by in case they needed to get out their pieces of rope to help pull the ship free then realized that was too simple. The mechanisms of the space ship would do the rest to free it.

The aliens appeared before the boys who were standing there watching them when each of the aliens beamed something from their one eye to each of the brothers. They felt a kinship with the aliens as the aliens disappeared into the space ship with the hatch closing after them. The thrusters did just what they had been told would happen. The space ship lifted a bit, rocked itself then moved out of the mountain. The jet propulsion kicked in and the space ship twirled and in a flash it was gone. Peter and Andy just stood there looking out at the bright, blue sky that they had not seen in many days. They did not know how long they had been inside the mountain whether it was days or weeks. It all seemed like a dream to them now.

There was no need for them to say anything as they could communicate without words. Still Andy said, "I feel different somehow. What do you suppose they did to us when they shone the light from their eye into ours?" Peter replied that he also felt strange. He said out loud, "Somehow I can think more clearly. It feels like I know a whole lot more than I can imagine."

With this, they stepped out and began the climb down the side of the mountain never looking back to the hole that was slowly closing behind them. Their walk through the mountain was finished. The downhill walking went more quickly than they thought. As they reached the lowlands, Peter said to Andy, "When we were talking about what we wanted to become when we grew up, I said an astronaut. Now I know I am going to be a marine biologist."

As they looked around, there before them was their father. He never looked so good in his life to the boys.

They ran to him hugging him. The dad could not imagine the relief he felt holding his two sons in his arms. He picked up his cell phone to call his wife to report that a miracle had just happened in their lives. Peter and Andy smiled at each other knowing just what Mom was hearing and telling their sister, Abby, their brother, Nate, and their cousin, Allie, that Peter and Andy were located and were on their way home.

Edwards Brothers, Inc.
Thorofare, NJ USA
March 17, 2012